The Friendship Tree

Kathy Caple

Holiday House / New York

In memory of my grandparents

Text and illustrations copyright © 2000 by Kathy Caple
All Rights Reserved
Printed in the United States of America
First Edition
Reading Level: 2.5

Library of Congress Cataloging-in-Publication Data
Caple, Kathy.
The Friendship Tree / by Kathy Caple.—1st Ed.
p. cm.
Summary: Blanche and Otis, two friends who are sheep,
enjoy each other's company from the autumn
through the winter to the spring.
ISBN 0-8234-1376-4
[1. Sheep—Fiction. 2. Trees—Fiction.
3. Friendship—Fiction.]
I. Title.
PZ7.C17368B1 2000
[E]—dc21   99-39043
CIP
AC

Contents

Leaves

Blanche was visiting Otis
in his backyard.
"Fall is here," said Otis.
"Leaves are dropping off my tree."
"You are lucky," said Blanche.
"I only have a pine tree.
It has needles.
It stays green all year."

When leaves fall off,"
said Otis,
"I have to rake them."
"I love to rake,"
said Blanche.
"You can help me,"
said Otis.
"Yippee," said Blanche.

5

Blanche and Otis raked five big piles.

"Now what?" asked Blanche.

"I put them in big bags.

I carry them to the dump," said Otis.

"It is a shame," said Blanche,
"to waste good leaves."
"You can put them
  in your yard," said Otis.

Blanche carried the leaves
to her yard.

"Oh dear," she said.

"This is not the same as seeing
leaves fall from my own tree."

Blanche went inside.

Otis thought of a surprise.

He got some string.
He put the leaves in
the bags.

At last
he was ready.

Otis knocked on the door.

"Close your eyes," said Otis.

He led Blanche to the pine tree.

He pulled the string.

"You can open your eyes now,"
he said.
The leaves drifted down
from the pine tree.
"Why Otis," said Blanche,
"that is the nicest surprise."

The Storm

It was stormy.
Blanche and Otis
were playing checkers.
Suddenly there was a loud boom.
"Thunder," said Blanche.

Outside, the wind picked up.
The branches on Otis's tree
were bending and swaying.
There was lightning.
There was more thunder.
The rain came down fast.
Just then, the lights went out.

"Come on," said Otis.
"We'd better move to the cellar."

Otis and Blanche found flashlights.
"It's spooky down here,"
said Blanche.

The storm got worse.

It shook the house.

BAM! They heard a crash.

"What was that?" cried Blanche.

"Maybe the roof blew off,"
said Otis.

"What if my house blew away?"
said Blanche.

All night long,

Otis and Blanche tried not to worry.

Finally they fell asleep.

When they woke up,

the sun was out.

Otis and Blanche ran upstairs.

"It was not my roof," said Otis.

"My house is still here,"
said Blanche.

"My tree," said Otis softly.

"There will be no more shade,"
said Blanche.

"Birds used to nest in it," said Otis.

"It was very old."

Otis remembered all the good things about his tree.

"Things will never be the same," he said.

Blanche squeezed Otis's hoof.

There was nothing more to say.

Christmas

Many weeks had passed.

There was a big pile of wood

on Otis's back porch.

Snow was everywhere.

"You can't tell where the big tree was,"

said Blanche.

"I know," said Otis sadly.

The next
morning,
Otis heard
a knock.
He opened
the door.
There was
a large crate.

He looked
inside.
"A baby
pine tree!"
he said.
He saw a note.

Dear Otis,
Christmas is one week away.
Here is a pine tree.
You can decorate it.
Feed it and water it.
In the spring,
I will help you plant it.
          Your friend,
          Blanche

Otis set the tree by the window.

Later Blanche came over.

They hung shiny balls
and paper snowflakes.

Otis smiled.

"Winter is a lot brighter now,"
he said.

"Good," said Blanche.

"Now I have to go home.

I am working

on your Christmas present."

"Oh dear," said Otis.

"I need a present for Blanche."

He went into town.

He looked around.

"I have an idea," said Otis.

On Christmas Eve,

Blanche came over.

She did not bring a present.

Maybe she forgot, thought Otis.

Otis and Blanche ate dinner.

They sang songs.

"Here is your present," said Otis.

Blanche opened it.

"A snow globe," she said.

"It has a pine tree inside."

Blanche shook the globe.

Tiny red and orange leaves
swirled around the tree.
"A leaf globe," said Blanche.
"I love it.
Now put on your coat and hat."

Blanche led Otis into his backyard.
"There are two chairs
where the tree used to be,"
said Otis.
"I made them out of logs
from your tree," said Blanche.
"They are perfect," said Otis.

Then Otis and Blanche
made two snow sheep
to sit in the chairs.
It was the best Christmas ever.

Spring

"Spring is here," said Blanche.
"It's time to plant your pine tree."

Otis and Blanche carried the tree
outside and planted it.

"It looks great," said Blanche.

"In no time, it will be tall."

Otis went back into his house.

He looked where the tree had been.

Then he looked outside.

"Maybe it is too soon," said Otis.

That night,

Otis could not sleep.

"Maybe it is too cold

for the tree."

Otis tiptoed out to check on it.

"Brr, it is cold," said Otis.

He put a blanket around the tree.

"This will keep you warm," he said.

The next morning,
Otis went to see Blanche.
"Please help me
take the tree back inside,"
he said.
"It is an indoor tree."
"I'll get a shovel," said Blanche.

When they got to the tree,
a bird was sitting in it.
Another one flew down
and sat beside it.
They began to sing.
"They want to build a nest
in your tree," said Blanche.

"That means birds will sleep
in its branches at night,"
said Otis.
"It will not be cold.
It will not be lonely.
It has birds."
Otis and Blanche watched
the birds build a nest.

Before long, there were
five smooth eggs in the nest.

A few weeks later,

the nest was filled with baby birds.

"It is like the little pine tree
   has always been there," said Otis.
"I know," said Blanche.

Otis and Blanche

went to the chairs

and sat down.

Everything was just right.